AF249352

ALSO BY MORGAN BELL

Collections
Sniggerless Boundulations
Laissez Faire
Intersection Control: Collected Works

Short stories
Midnight Daisy
The Switch
Don't Pay The Ferryman
Trouble By The Jarful
A Deer In The Shunting Yard
Boxcar Dreams

Anthologies
(as editor)
Sproutlings: A Compendium of Little Fictions

Morgan Bell is an author of short fiction from Newcastle, Australia. Her books include *Sniggerless Boundulations*, *Laissez Faire*, and *Intersection Control: Collected Works*. She is a qualified technical writer, creative writing teacher, and editor of *Sproutlings: A Compendium of Little Fictions*.

Idiomatic, For The People is her first collection of poetry.

It is also her first full-length 'concept album' style project-book. The work was conceived, planned, and executed with a set-theme – survival mechanisms – in mind. The project took one year to complete.

Idiomatic,
For The People

Idiomatic,
For The People

Morgan Bell

Gunsmith Doll
2018

First Printing: 2019

ISBN 9-780244-4577-61

Gunsmith Doll
Sydney, Australia
www.gunsmithdoll.com

Cover deign by Gunsmith Doll
Interior illustrations by Nick Vuimin
Ink blots attributed to Shtiel

For Samantha:
my sister,
my first friend,
and
my ideal distillation of
integrity
and
good

if the wind changes, you'll stay like that
                              — ancient familial proverb

pale in the flare light
the scared light cracks and disappears
and leads the scorched ones here
and everywhere no one cares
the fire is spreading
and no one wants to speak about it
                              — chris cornell

⊕

fig. a renewed energy after a period of fatigue
— n. second wind

o

fig. to rest as to be able to resume breathing normally after
stopping breathing momentarily from fear, surprise, or a
taxing activity
— v. catch your beath

.

.

‡

≡

It's not poetry, it's formatting.

.   ⊕   .

It's not sentences, it's the nearest approximation to the
constellation of word-marmalade that curdles inside the
mind of someone locked in survival mode.

o o

.

Contents

FIGHT

Fight 1: Hammer it home

hammer it home to him: never root an 'it' or homo man, never
enter the rear, hone in on the meat-mitten tit, renovate vain
terror, have no honor in the naïve mate, to taint, to tame
eat the rim, over hormone trim, have more non-men
ram the iron main-vein, earn the invert he-rooter
one orientation, to retire home, rotten homo
no harm in tarnation, torment them here
orate the hate rime – reiteration time
revert to the overt even in their era
mention their intent to the otter
amen, hit the maven riven
tear at her throat over an
intimate motion moan
venerate the mother
either meet me
here – or –
a r r i v e
t h e r
e

a corset is a fortress, my armour, mi amor
              the vixen
                      you want
              I want you   to cut
              to thrash in barbs
                      me

underwire, boosts the breast, plate
              it
                      up

                      you are
              I am
                      the monster
                      I
              you
                      better run

Fight 3: Too quiet loudly

i

Yesterday it was too quiet. I had Nothing to say, so loudly. Nothing is the coyote's wiles, when he's running down the road. And the Nothing doesn't matter. When his eyes are screaming. And yours are obscured by the screen.

ii

Last night a pink diamond came pouncing out your mouth. It was buried in your larynx. But when you started to fuss about, it could no longer be accepted. A bouquet of trumpets flurried: there is Nothing to announce.

iii

While I slept, the TV static sizzled like fire doused in water. The gestures of a shaggy collie became so fuzzy at the edges. I could not control the contrast. And the thought-casting clicking. Skippy. Would not stop.

iv

Before dawn a message in a bottle washed up on the shore of Nowhereland. The air was frigid. My fingers pruned - they had no choice; it helped them keep their grip under water. Or so I'm told. The slowly unrolled paper was cacophonously blank.

v

When an anvil drops on TNT, one me says
to the other me, turn down the TV. Silence
cannot compete with your hard-won noise.
So, I find inside my head I speak to myself
in a language no-one else can understand.

vi

The human ear is estranged from the earth's
hum, a bigger Nothing, yet somehow still
measured. All spinsters are snitches. And
witches. And bitches. And thin lips get
stiches. And Nothing gets ditches, in earth.

vii

The day after I escaped being 'a lot of fun', I
realized my clothes had gotten louder the
more I faded away. Everyone knows baby-
spice doesn't sing, and isn't really a baby.
She's a sexy kitten in her terrible twenties.
Or she has to pretend to be.

viii

During autumn my tongue grew fat from the
hard swallow of too many couches. All the
thoughts are jostling each other out of the
way. They call each other worms as they
push back, shoulder-to-shoulder. If they
could shout out to you, you would see they
agree, that you will be you and I will be me.

the way to crush a man is not
to drag a heel across his goals
but stomp him, make him wah wah wah
and coyly push the pull

the way to crush a man is not
to raze him to stubbled ruin
but shave your face and shave your feet
and gently drive the screw in

the way to keep my body safe
is to not let my lash peel off
to never let my hair go flat
to stoop yet seem much straightened

the way to keep my body safe
is always to exaggerate
to reek of tropes in havoc's wake
to shush with sheen and common place

of melon calves and meat-bone hands
the level-best giantess will
rest her elbows on his neck
she knows how to crush a man

Fight 5: The jackal and the hyena

What you're about to see here is an ambush in the wild savannah of the vast Southport Centrelink. The lion has already finished eating the nutrient-rich organs. The liver. The heart. What's left is nothing notable. So, he wanders off. When the lion is no longer visible, the black-backed jackal appears and tries to enjoy a meal of left-overs.

You got to put up with them cocksuckers in there. Is he bringing out that form or what, security guard?

From a distance, a pack of hyenas spies the black-backed jackal as she pops her head up from the scraps. There's no way a black-backed jackal would have been on those scraps if the lion still wanted them. Little jackals aren't going to eat anything near a lion. A lion would crush them with one swoop of a paw. So, they wait until the coast is clear.

I was seeing why those cunts were
stuffing my payment around.

> The hyenas also want to grab the scraps. Lion
>
> scraps are perfect for the musculature of a hye-
>
> na jaw, which is even stronger than that of a
>
> lion. Hyenas have thick, robust teeth, perfect
>
> for crushing the bones that lions leave behind.

Yeah well that's fucked, that's what
it is, that's fucked, fucked up centrelink motherfuckers.

> Hyenas don't pursue jackals to eat them. Jack-
>
> als are too quick to catch and don't have a lot
>
> of meat on them.

I'm not in the right mood, at this
point of time.

> When they do chase jackals, it is to chase them
>
> away from kills, after they fight amongst them-
>
> selves over their find.

And now I've got to fucking deal
with that shit. Who's gonna pay my
rent?

Seeing the hyenas benefit from the lion's hunt shouldn't give the impression that hyenas and lions have a commensal relationship.

Three hundred and fifty dollars... like tony abbott, the motherfucker, he can't even house people.

The lion readily leaps back onto the scene, scattering the hyenas, when the noise of the hyenas haranguing the jackal piques his interest for the kill once again. The scene made him wonder if he might have left good food behind.

... them cunts to give me a house. He can't even do that, tony abbott.

The hyenas recognise that the lion will claim ownership over whatever he wants, and simply take it. Nothing in nature goes to waste. And everything of value goes to the most powerful first.

Do you know how frustrating that is?

We never see hyenas challenge a lion. When we see hyenas taking a kill for themselves, they're actually swiping it from the jackal, not the lion.

______**DO YOU HAVE A JOB???????**____________

_______YOU HAVE A JOB??????_____________

_________HAVE A JOB?????_______________

____________A JOB???___________________

____________JOB??____________________

___________HUB?___________________

__________JAY BUD?_______________

_________BOAB YOB?______________

________JAVA-HUED BOD?________

_______HAD YOU JOY DUE HOOD?

Quote the hyena

What we're watching between the lion and the hyena isn't a conflict at all. Grabbing the bones out from under the lion's nose, is actually a case of leftover scavenging.

FLIGHT

 # Rain on tin

Rain on tin. I tether him to a titan home. Hem
him in. Rein on mammoth horn. Roam over to
tie him to that vent. Hear that roar. Arrive in
time to heave the earth. Oh Romeo moon. Oh
terran Thor. Oh Eve on a thin throne. Minor
hero. Hoar veneer too rare to entertain her.
Invite them to maintain her attention. Leave a
tiara – not too ovate not too ornate - in
the ante-room. Not too trite. Here in the
intra-aero tear in time. I hear the orator
tame her to retrieve her heathen heart.
Neither a totem, nor a haven nor a move
to atone. A time-intermittent, ever vehement
retort. Motion to the ether. Her native north.
He met in the torrent to move the
vane antenna one teem at a time. I ate an
aviator heron - over the rotten raven -
at a teatime in the tremor tent that month.
He – Heath or Norman – tore at the methane
aromata. The tear. The oath, too torn. Tie it
to their honor. Earn her ire. Moth on hive.
A marionette hint in the tart trim rite. A
toothier rat never ran on more than their
hare. Or a mite on an ant, or a moth on
a hornet hive. Invite him to either orient or
tether her to the air-horn. Veer into the eve.
Not too hot to vent, near motte or rent. I
remain in the tar, the mire. Therma to term.
The remover to remover. An eminent trove.

Flight 2: Distraction code

```
>>>>>              >>>>>              >>>>>
  >>>>>              >>>>>              >>>>>
    >>>>>              >>>>>              >>>>>
  >>>>>              >>>>>              >>>>>
>>>>>              >>>>>              >>>>>
```

```
F:\>type

Give  the  people  more  of  what  they  really
want.txt


    <held un=
    "The pop projectile"
            >Leaves them distracted
    </held>


    <said un=
    "The scattered smithereens"
            >Keeps them busied
    </said>


    <kept un=
    "The tight-stitched pocket"
            >Sees them rummaged
    </kept>


    <seen un=
    "The away-getting of it"
            >Holds them stalled
    </seen>
```

Dearest Chauncey,

I write to you with great astonishment and regret for ever having mustered the will to embark on this errant journey. You will never believe, Chauncey, the encounter I had today when I occasioned upon a dark man of little means while touring the Protectorate. You simply will not be able to fathom the staggering pluck and bottle of this brazen fellow. So the duty falls on me to lay it out for you plainly —

We can provide you with no accommodation, he said, Chauncey. None whatsoever.
I had the agency to protest, yes. Bold as a sap-sucking aphid, he was. And as far afield. I politely reminded him the same cultivated crops that I owned are those upon which sugar cane with a long spoon he did sup. Disposable was my dominion to him. He demanded his due! Can you believe it, Chauncey! Eager for constraint, I told him, this is why we instituted

a colony in this god-forsaken
handle of a place. But would he desist
from this ungrateful tirade?
back and he'll ride to the deep blue
sea. Gratitude was not in his nature.
are an institution, I told him. And
his response? A mere shrug.
he protested. As though I didn't
have better places to be, people to
The protectorates are a damn
institution, Chauncey. You
from your protectorates. I fear I
am losing my mind out here. Is not
concentrated institution? Is this
not what we were told, and learnt?
Move on! Or was that move on in?
Were we moving away from our own
it was a mess to flee, or an example to
help be? All I have been taught,
in time and shrunk in place and
become so distorted it can only
truth that jailbirds - not so black
as they are painted - prefer to
ised. An idea suddenly unrecognizable

fire-in-the-frying-pan-

Get a devil on beggar-

Houses, big houses,

I don't want you here,

join in finer settlements.

know your settlements

land-locked labour a

Messy country?

neck of the woods because

or know, has now stretched

poorly exemplify the

quail away, institutional-

yet chillingly familiar. The wretch ruined me, Chauncey.
I am desperate to close my eyes and
draw in oatmeal and tobacco. To settle back and subdivide
sweet cotton realms at the 22nd
parallel. Vast regions of such taupe, tan, and toady
sand. But, alas, this charmless man had
sugared the tank and gone sold me up the river. To an
unsettled slammer. That's how I felt.
He treated me like a common vandal. Unentitled,
poaching on his vacant virgin ground.
This from someone born on the wrong side of the blanket.
A blatant attempt to wring my withers.
Note, it was vacant when the XY coordinates were
fixed unto the master map. Just a vector
through an axis. His last words, you broke me, you bought
me, rang in my ears. I felt I was in a
vortex. I would never be the same. Zero sum game, it was,
now the devils know I am not long dead.

Flight 4: My thoughts

My thoughts trail off . . . trail off . . . trail off . . . trail off . . .

My thoughts recoil . . . recoil . . . recoil . . . recoil . . . recoil . . . recoil . . . recoil . . .

My thoughts are a staccato jerk-buck-brittle carbon-circuit-breaker clap . . . a perfect pocket on a concrete skirt . . . a wicked mental echo . . . a chaotic, yet early-onset, rapier wit . . . to clog it is to lick it, bit-by-bit, shrill a coconut down at the crackerjack split

I knew a woman who I thought spoke almost entirely in riddles, a string of contrary statements. It was incomprehensible.·········¶

But then one day I found out she was covering for her best friend who didn't know the truth about anything, even though he thought he did.

She had to keep both versions of reality alive in her mind, like two near untranslatable languages on the tip of her tongue. And sometimes they crossed over.·····¶

And the man would scream and shout. The other version of the story stung his skin and made him small.¶

So she blocked out all the windows to stop it from ever coming in.·········¶

FREEZE

Here's the thing about being read, being read is being heard. And that's a little bit daunting for me, the idea that someone might actually listen, or indeed hear. It's why I find writing poetry so hard. For some people it's not hard, it's the easiest form of writing, because you can just let it flow out of you. Bleed on the page. When I think about why this is so hard for me, like really think, I realise it comes down to two things, mainly. One is it's hard because I feel bad for asking for your attention when the focus is solely me. I feel guilty for holding your attention for so long if you're not getting anything out of it. Ever the consummate performer. If I am going to monopolise your time I need to make it worth your while. And what is an incoherent rambling worth to someone so far outside of my own experience. You won't be able to relate to me. You will get

I am
not
here

bored, think I'm self-involved (which I am, but I hate for people to know it, I put a lot of effort into maintaining that façade), and leave with a sense of being cheated that you invested your valuable time in paying me attention. And two, I find it very hard to write in first person, in any format. Write how you talk. Some valuable advice from a poet friend. But what if the things you say are so very different to the things you think. If what I say is a construct, then is transcribing it to the page completely worthless without the context of the delivery method. What I say is modulated by how, when, and where I say it. Of who I say it to. But the page is an anonymous audience to calibrate to. To invent to.

Freeze 2: On the page

this only makes sense on the page
   I only make sense on the page
      if only my existence made sense

I only exist on the page
   this only exists in me
      I make this only exist in me

I make sense only to me
     my sense of myself only exists on the page
      I only exist to make sense of this

the only extant
   my only sentient
     self only present
       only
         only
           only
             only
             only
               only
             only
            only
          only
           only

1. Hands /hændz/ (sweet)

a. The act of looking ahead and seeing all the time in the world. Having it all to pluck at whim.

b. A naïve juicy berry. Illness is her odd little imaginary friend who lives in the barrel with the boarded-up windows, rotting, pitted.

2. Light of day /laɪt əv deɪ/ (clear)

a. A glass-brick wall with two distinctly obscured black masses. A thick consuming tar beside the still ink-dark pond of always.

b. When Illness is an unfortunate township slowly seen sinking as one swims amongst the lily-pads.

3. Feet /fiːt/ (spooked)

a. My buttons trying to devour me and my anti-perspirant poisoning my mind.

b. A scarecrow of yellow malaise getting settled in the crow-patch.

c. When Illness is a gloating chain-gang guard scoring my skin with lashings of nickle and aluminium.

4. Turkey /tɜːʳki/ *(masochism)*

> **a.** The act of apologizing for being late when I have an allergic reaction to knowing the time.
> **b.** A tough leather of excuses.
> **c.** When Illness is a goose-bump flayed from red raw chicken flesh.

5. Fish /fɪʃ/ *(detachment)*

> **a.** Clock arms frozen in time, seized and sedentary, with its hands (and feet) amputated from neuropathy.

6. Shoulder /ʃoʊldəʳ/ *(forbidding)*

> **a.** The quadrant of Space where Carrie Fisher was strangled by her own bra, because enough already, I can't focus on you while I'm trying to figure out how to manage this.
> **b.** When I am the grasshopper who didn't think time would go on quite so long.

7. Blood /blʌd/ *(deliberate)*

> **a.** My lack of time for you, because I lost my homeostasis and my blood is full of candy canes, and preservation is my main concern.
> **b.** When Illness is a countdown.

on a mattress
down
with my ragdoll arms
down
in a too-empty room
down
beside a two-bar heater
down
under a lei carnation
down
beneath the layers
down
in my lair
down
among the half-packed boxes
down
below the sea-ice mountain
down
amid the glacial
down
stuck in a long layover
down
beside sharp red alarm
down
in the too-far moment
down
cooling lava
down
almost stops

this is a country of fabric℃™ ⠿ woven from the natural things in life ⠿ made from scratch & fibre ⠿ we wear it because we should ⠿ our low of lows, these sloppy joes ⠿ mop the panic soaked, rupt and broke, ⠿ deaf of tone, lashing the lone ⠿ threads we don't want in our fabric℃™ ⠿ the children, the children, those nancy minds ⠿ as tommy learns the mary mould ⠿ and molly mimics what he finds ⠿ then when it's all over ⠿ farewell we, these lifted shirts ⠿ the fabric℃™ is more re-strictive ⠿ than it really needs to be ⠿ muncher divers are the reason ⠿ for upstairs gardeners ⠿ on the ground, the truth is ⠿ the fabric℃™ is in season ⠿ all year round ⠿

FAWN

 # Mine on the moon

meet   (((((((((her there, at   the mine on the moon)))))))

(((((((((((((((((((((((((((   ))))))))))))))))))))))))))))))))

her((((((((heart too eaten   to remain on the earth)))))))

there,   ((((((((((((((to tame   her naïve air, he met her))))

at((((((((((((the river arm   the torrent ran to him)))))))

(((((((((((((((((((((((((((   ))))))))))))))))))))))))))))))

the((ammonite entreat her   to thieve an emotive term))

mine   ((((((heave to remove   the iron in the ore))))))))))))

on(((((((((the roam home,   have him mention her name

the((((((((time to hear her   over in a moment)))))))))))))

moon   ((((((((((over motte   near riven rent, he earnt her

Beat the finger of the hand
    that feeds you
        from every pie.
           Beat it with an

                        iron

gutting wrench.
    The under-thumbed
        are living
           hammed

                        fist

to mouth. The
    tight fisted upper hand
        slowly goes to bone.
           To spill his guts

                        in a

ham cast dye.
    A thumb in the eye
        of the long arm of
           the law. Tipping the

                        velvet

he hams up his
    strings between his
        finger tips. No
           beat down -

                        glove

in hand - with garters for guts. He says,
don't spill the glory.

Fawn 3: The four blues

[WRAP]

•

Her
head held
back, she
overheard
blue noise
running
from an
exsanguinated
tap. It was
impossible
to tell if
the cord
had been
pulled from
around
her neck,
because
there were
no signs,
and
no dotted
lines,
just
a tight
and
dressy
feeling.

[HACK]

•

There's a
lumberjack
somewhere,
chopping
in waves,
at a
stiff
jarring
pace, but
he's
too short
to make
a sound.
Far from
the fell,
his
sprayed
splinters
lodge in
a parachute
of
bruise-blue
sky
and ink
begins
to
trickle.

[TAP]

•

Near my
wrist,
the low
swollen
drop,
that hangs
heavy in the
chamber,
prepares to
fall, while
the drip
before it
drowns a
slow death
inside my
vein,
turning blue
behind my
skin. I
cannot stop
how they
are drawn
through
the tube,
not for
all the ink
welling.

[SHUT]

•

My sunken
eyes, unable
to resist
the weight
of languor,
search
the chamber
for
a nightdress,
which is
just
a daydress
undistressed.
I labour in
the difference,
even with the
air hypoxic,
and the
echo chills
too shallow,
in this
deep
well, light
returning,
unabsorbing,
a blue way of
being.

*P*aper

A friend is the best possession.

*C*hina

A best friend is a possessive dog who enjoys a short leash and a tight chain. She has a strong need to rollover, sit, beg, obey, and shake.

*C*rystal

A dog is a possession, a belonging, an asset, an object, that moves, where you let it, where you allow it, where you instruct it, until it doesn't.

*L*inen

A possessed dog is someone you rescue and allocate a very specific location in your house, or sometimes not in your house at all, just looking through the window to the life you lead inside, all the while fearing she wants to bite you

Silverware

She is someone who can't get any work done with your puppy at her heels! She liked that he could bring a dog to heel, and pant at her leg, and cool her head. But as soon as he was hot on her heels, she wanted to call off the dogs. It was clear she was barking up the wrong tree by trying to catch the bone he'd been throwing her.

Wood

A short friendship is a dog of a thing. It was a dog-act but he was dying to leave. He dogged her, and left like a dog in the night, just like the low-down dirty dog that he was.

Copper

The best trick is throwing a sausage down a hallway and watching her go to work. After his short friend said 'she's a real dog mate' he brought out the Chum and the Pal. He was done with it. Left it looking like a dog's breakfast down there. But every dog has its day, and no matter how dog-eared the bone-trap, he could still see there's life in the old dog yet. All he knows now is, you're dog meat bitch.

Bronze

A best friend's man is not so friendly when asking 'why don't you smile?' He's off the leash. The call of the wild and the scent of the heat left him thrilled as a dog with two tails giving chase to a fine piece of skirt. He tells you about the school of hard knocks, but he doesn't have a dog in this fight, due to all the wagging, he didn't learn a thing.

Terracotta

A dog manship is the simmering resentment of always letting sleeping dogs lie, and chasing your tail until you are looking for a dog to kick. And that dog is yourself. But sticking the boot in makes you wake from this nightmare covered with fleas. And you find yourself making the biting remark 'why bark if you have dogs?' to your loyal receptionist.

Diamond

The best dogship is short. Because why buy the bark if you can get the bite for free? It ends with, 'Do you take this dog to love, honour, and obey?' And 'I now pronounce you man and dog.' And 'Sit, woman, sit. Good wife.' The fear is, if it's too common, every man and his wife will be there.

Fawn 5: Her spun yarns

In a glimmering lamé room, among the golden alligator leaf, in swirling pastel teal and pink, there is a mirror with no reflection. By cupboards filled with cosy cashmere musk and lemon silk, the damask walls are almost too opulent to behold; by Faberge himself they might have been papered, in painterly olive and amber. The sun's rays pick out flecks of linseed from the cadmium. They are known as linen, the textiles made from flax. There is a woman, separated by a pane, that can be seen when looking close in the mirror's teloscopic view. She is yarning on a hill of sweetgum cover.

At the base of a satin-walnut maple, there are berry-buds among the hedgerow. There, in the cobalt and cerulean hues of a slant confetti rain, by hook or by crook, the spinster keeps on yarning llama fleece. She hums a tune of solitude and light. It is a wordless mournful song of disappearing from sight. In her muffled howling over leaving no memory of her shape, she becomes the llama separated from the heard. Her eyes spill drops of pleading. You can read them. You don't want this. Go from here.

At first you didn't see her, she is so good at her job, separating the darkness from the shadows, to store it out of frame, with all the deformed fibres, she plucks from her spun yarns.

Acknowledgements

Beyond the more overt influences of E. E. Cummings, Gertrude Stein, and Lewis Carroll, I read an incredible amount of contemporary poetry collections in the year I spent composing this book. It was a year of rediscovering poetry. The joy of reading cleverly constructed phrases, hidden secrets, and raw expression. It was an inspiration to be reminded of all the non-conformist ways words can be arranged on a page.

I would like to acknowledge the submission guidelines for the Subbed In 2018 Chapbook Prize that gave me a framework to launch from – the idea of being in the margins of this 'patriarchal hellscape' – and rekindled my enthusiasm for analysing the queer-activist term 'heter-onormative' from which many of my anagrams and acrostics were centred on. I also acknowledge the Not Very Quiet women's journal Issue 3, September 2018, submission guidelines, where ekphrastic stimu-lus/provocation was Grace Cossington Smith Interior with wardrobe mirror 1955 and Fay Zwicky, 'Border Crossings', 2000. 'Her spun yarns' is a reworked piece originally conceived in response to that stimulus, and the sensibilities extolled in the 'Provocation', as selected by Lisa Brock-well, have no doubt peppered all you read here.

'The jackal and the hyena' contains quoted and paraphrased text from 'Battle' Between a Lion and Hyenas Isn't What it Seems by Andrea Vale published August 4, 2017 in National Geographic, and from tran-scribed audio of a viral video depicting a clip from an Australian TV current affairs interview outside Southport Centrelink QLD, circa March 2015, uploaded to YouTube both as 'Aboriginal calls out tony Abbott on today tonight' by Faze Loomifuckinaty and 'Fucked Up CentreLink Motherfuckers' by Thomas Nick Karamzalis.

Thank you to illustrator Nick Vuimin for creating the custom draw-ings of 'survival-response' rabbits that introduce each section. Thank you to Magdalena Ball for her guidance and mentorship, and to Dael Allison and Joanna Atherfold Finn for being early readers.

'One of the most galling things about living with depression is the concentration-loss inhibiting your ability to read long-form works. When novel-reading becomes a frustrating endeavour, short-form poetry is a unique comfort. Poets: saving my sanity, one superb use of negative space at a time.' - Morgan Bell, 2018

The titles I scoured over and studied and dipped in and out of while creating Idiomatic, For The People:

Intact by Anne Walsh
Parenthetical Bodies by Allison Gallagher
Sing Out When You Want Me by Kerri Shying
Engraft by Michele Seminara
Unmaking Atoms by Magdalena Ball
Paint Peels, Graffiti Sings by Jan Dean
The Duties of a Cat by Jenny Blackford
Straight Lines by Sanna Peden
Comfort Food by Ellen Van Neervan
Tropeland by Rob Walker
The Non-Sequitur of Snow by Shari Kocher
The Future by Neil Hilborn
Wild Hundreds by Nate Marshall
Calenture by Lindsay Tuggle
Where The Lost Things Go by Anne Casey
And My Heart Crumples Like a Coke Can by Ali Whitelock
The Bloomin' Notions of Other & Beau by Toby Fitch
Fairweather's Raft by Dael Allison
The Sly NightCreatures of Desire by Debi Hamilton
Common Sexual Fantasies, Ruined by Rachael Briggs
Beatific Toast by Anna Forsyth
Slated Voices by Mavis Gulliver & Jan Fortune
Vitus Dreams by Adam Craig
Sublime Planet by Magdalena Ball and Carolyn Howard-Johnson
High Wire Step by Magdalena Ball
Awake At The Wheel by Berndt Sellheim
Milk and Honey by Rupi Kaur
The Sun and Her Flowers by Rupi Kaur
Rigor-tortoise: 2018 Newcastle Poetry At The Pub anthology
Brew: 30 Years of Poetry at the Pub Newcastle
The World's Wife by Carol Ann Duffy
The World Doesn't End by Charles Simic

www.ingramcontent.com/pod-product-compliance
Lightning Source LLC
Chambersburg PA
CBHW032127050726

47590CB00008B/2997